FULL COURT Dreams

BY JAKE MADDOX

illustrated by Tuesday Mourning

text by Val Priebe

Librarian Reviewer
Chris Kreie
Media Specialist, Eden Prairie Schools, MN
MS in Information Media, St. Cloud State University, MN

Reading Consultant
Mary Evenson
Middle School Teacher, Edina Public Schools, MN
MA in Education, University of Minnesota

STONE ARCH BOOKS
Minneapolis   San Diego

Impact Books are published by Stone Arch Books
151 Good Counsel Drive, P.O. Box 669
Mankato, Minnesota 56002
www.stonearchbooks.com

Library of Congress Cataloging-in-Publication Data
Maddox, Jake.
    Full Court Dreams / by Jake Maddox; illustrated by Tuesday
Mourning.
      p. cm. — (Impact Books — A Jake Maddox Sports Story)
      ISBN 978-1-4342-0469-1 (library binding)
      ISBN 978-1-4342-0519-3 (paperback)
      [1. Basketball—Fiction.] I. Mourning, Tuesday, ill. II. Title.
PZ7.M25643Ful 2008
[Fic]—dc22   2007031261

Summary: It's the day of basketball tryouts, and Annie overslept! She
can't believe she's running late on the most important day of the year.
Last year, Annie and her best friends, Megan and Emma, were cut from
the team. Of course, the school mean girls, Sarah and Dani, made it.
But this year there's a new coach, and Annie's been practicing her heart
out. Annie is determined to make the team this year, and she isn't going
to let anything stand in her way!

Art Director: Heather Kindseth
Graphic Designer: Kay Fraser

1 2 3 4 5 6 13 12 11 10 09 08

Printed in the United States of America

TABLE OF Contents ✳

Chapter 1
THE FIRST DAY

Annie sat straight up in her bed. "Oh, thank goodness," she whispered, relieved. "It was only a dream."

In her dream, the roster for this year's seventh-grade basketball team had been posted. It was a nightmare. Her name hadn't been on the list!

Annie rubbed her eyes and squinted at her alarm clock. The time, 6:49 a.m., glowed back at her in big red numbers.

"No!" exclaimed Annie. "Not today!" She jumped out of bed, suddenly wide awake.

She couldn't believe she had slept in on the one day she actually wanted to go to school.

Today was the first day of basketball tryouts. Annie had planned to get up early to make sure she had everything she needed. Instead, she had woken up nearly twenty minutes late.

I'm already screwing up, thought Annie. This is a really bad sign.

Annie hurried to get ready. She took a fast shower. Then she got dressed. She barely paid attention to the clothes she put on. She quickly pulled her hair back into a ponytail.

Finally, she made sure that her backpack was full of the things she'd need for tryouts. Then she headed downstairs.

Annie hurried down the stairs and ran into the kitchen. Her thoughts were still racing.

Her mom and her baby brother, Jack, were in the kitchen when Annie got there. A bowl of cereal was waiting on the table.

Annie's mom took one look at her face and smiled. "It's okay. Don't worry," Mom said.

Annie sighed. "I hate being late!" she said. "Now I'm going to feel messed up for the rest of the day."

"Honey, calm down," her mom said. "Eat some cereal and I'll get Jack ready to go."

"I'm so nervous," Annie said.

Mom said, "Annie, you are going to do great today. You have worked really hard. You were out practicing in that driveway every day. Your skills have definitely improved. And I think you're even a little taller than you were last year."

"Thanks, Mom," Annie said.

Mom smiled and added, "I'm so proud of you. No matter what happens this week, please remember that."

Just then, the phone rang. Annie jumped up to answer it. "Hello?" she said.

"Hi, sweetie!" It was Annie's dad, calling from his office. "Just wanted to call to say good luck today at your tryout," Dad said.

"Thanks, Dad," Annie said. "I better go. I'm going to be late."

"Good luck, honey," Dad said. "Bye!"

Annie hung up and shoveled cereal into her mouth. By the time she was done eating, her mom was waiting in the car.

Annie jumped into the car. She fastened her seatbelt as her mom backed down the driveway.

From his car seat, Jack yelled, "Go!" Annie smiled at her little brother.

Her mom smiled too. "You'll be just fine, Annie. You even have a new coach this year. It's a new beginning."

Annie sighed. She still felt off from waking up late. And she was really nervous about tryouts.

I hope my whole day isn't ruined, she thought.

Chapter 2
NERVOUS

Annie's mom pulled the silver car into the school parking lot. As Annie unbuckled her seat belt, her mom smiled.

"I'm proud of you," Mom said.

"I know. Thanks, Mom," Annie said, trying to smile back.

She grabbed her backpack. Then she waved goodbye to her mom and Jack and hopped out of the car.

Annie walked toward the school. As she neared the front doors, she spotted her two best friends, Emma and Megan, running toward her.

Emma and Megan couldn't be more different from each other. Emma was tall and strong, with long legs, long arms, and long hair. She laughed a lot.

Megan, on the other hand, was barely five feet tall. She had black hair and big brown eyes. She was quiet with most people, but not Emma and Annie.

Annie's friends looked excited when they reached her.

"The new coach is here!" said Emma.

"She's really young!" added Megan.

"Cool," said Annie. "Let's go see if we can find her."

The three girls walked past shouting boys and giggling girls toward the front doors of Kennedy Junior High School.

They headed straight to the main office. Through the glass window in the door, Annie could see a woman talking to Mrs. Brown, the school principal.

"Is that her?" asked Annie. She could hardly believe her eyes. The new coach looked more like Megan's older sister than someone old enough to coach them. She was short and had dark hair and blue eyes.

"Yep," replied Megan. "Her name is Ms. Jackson."

Then the bell rang. It was time to get to class. As they hurried down the hall, Megan said, "I hope she's nice. She looks nice. Do you guys think she'll be nice?"

office

"Calm down, Megan," Emma said with a laugh. "We have to get through the whole day first."

Annie knew Emma was more nervous than she was letting on. After all, the three friends had been cut from the basketball team last year. They didn't want that to happen again.

They walked quickly to their lockers. After grabbing their books for first period, they hurried to class.

Annie's mind wandered during her first class. She hardly paid attention to Mr. Hanson, even though he was her favorite teacher. Once, she didn't even notice when he was calling on her to answer a question. Her second period study hall and third period math class went by in a blur too.

Finally, it was time for lunch. Annie felt like she was in a daze. All she could think about were basketball tryouts.

Megan and Emma looked as nervous as Annie felt while they walked together toward the cafeteria. When they reached the lunchroom, the line was already pretty long.

Toward the front of the line, they heard a girl's voice say, "I can't wait until tryouts are over. I mean, I don't know why we have them anyway."

"Yeah," said another voice. "It's not like anyone else can even dribble in a straight line."

Emma stood on her tiptoes to look over the other people in line. "It's Sarah and Dani," she whispered.

Sarah and her best friend, Dani, had been starting players on last year's basketball team. They were pretty and popular. They both had long blond hair and blue eyes. Everyone liked them — or at least pretended to.

Sarah and Dani were also the meanest girls in the school. They made fun of just about everyone.

Sarah was pretty good at basketball, but Annie hadn't seen her at open gym or practicing at all over the summer. Dani wasn't as good as Sarah, but she had made the team last year anyway.

"Oh, no," groaned Megan. "I'm not hungry anymore."

"Come on, you guys. Just ignore them," said Annie.

Then Sarah spotted Emma. "Ooh, look at the giant!" she said loudly. "Think you'll make the team this year? I don't."

She and Dani laughed. Emma looked crushed.

"It's okay, Emma," Annie said. "She's just trying to make you nervous."

"Well, it's working," Emma said quietly.

After lunch was over, the second half of the day went by quickly. Annie had a history quiz in fifth period, a health lecture in sixth, and family studies class during seventh period. Nothing exciting.

When the final bell rang, Annie's stomach turned over.

Chapter 3
COACH JACKSON

The locker room was filled with nervous chatter when Annie, Megan, and Emma walked in after school.

With shaking hands, the girls opened their lockers and pulled out shorts, T-shirts, socks, and shoes. They dressed quickly and quietly.

From the other side of the lockers, Annie could hear Sarah saying, "Wow, nice shirt. I wonder if she got it at a garage sale."

"And did you see the band geeks over there? Who are they kidding?" Dani said.

"Let's go!" Emma whispered to Annie and Megan. The three girls were ready, so they slipped into the gym.

Their new coach was already there, talking to Coach Miller, the assistant basketball coach. Both coaches looked up at Megan, Emma, and Annie. The new coach smiled at them.

"Grab a ball and shoot around," said Coach Miller. "We'll start in about ten minutes." Soon, the gym was filled with the sound of bouncing basketballs.

After almost ten minutes had passed, Coach Jackson glanced at the clock on the wall. Then she walked to the locker room and opened the door.

"Anyone not out here by the time I count to five is cut!" she yelled. "One! Two! Three . . ." Then Sarah and Dani slowly walked out of the locker room.

Coach Jackson grabbed the whistle from around her neck and blew. She yelled, "Put the balls away! Five laps! And if I catch anyone cutting corners, I'll double it. Go!"

Megan put the ball in the wire cart. Then they started running.

"When you're done, make a circle in the middle for stretching," said the new coach.

Annie was nervous as she ran around the gym. She could hardly pay attention to how many laps she had run. On the third lap, she almost bumped into Sarah. Sarah didn't say anything, but she glared at Annie and sped up.

After everyone finished their laps, the girls gathered in a circle in the middle of the court. Each girl was breathing hard.

The coach walked into the middle of the circle. "Hi, girls," she said, smiling. "I'm Coach Jackson. I teach third grade. I played basketball in high school and college. I was a point guard."

She went on, "Not all of you will be here at the end of the week. I hate to cut anyone, but there are just too many of you trying out this year."

Coach Jackson looked around and said, "While you're here, you will follow my rules. I don't have very many of them, so it won't be hard. The first rule is you will try your best, no matter what, at all times. The second rule is that you'll always be a team player. Let's get started!"

Everyone stood up.

Annie looked at Megan. "She's tough," Megan whispered.

"I like her," Annie whispered back.

Coach Jackson clapped her hands and said, "Okay, everybody grab a ball and line up on the end line. We're going to do layups. Follow me."

Coach Jackson started dribbling toward the basket on the right side of the court. She dribbled in, made her layup, got her rebound, and then dribbled across to the left side. There, she made another layup.

Quickly, the girls lined up and followed Coach Jackson through the layup drill.

Annie and her friends ended up somewhere in the middle. Sarah and Dani were at the end.

Annie and her friends finished in time to watch Sarah and Dani slowly jog to the last basket and shoot layups. It didn't look like they were trying. Sarah didn't even make her shot.

When everyone was done, Coach Jackson shook her head. "Well, that was terrible," she said. "Do you all remember the first rule? The one about trying your hardest?"

The girls all nodded. Then Coach Jackson said, "Let's do this again. This time, if I catch anyone not hustling, or if you miss more than two shots, you have to run five more laps. Go!"

Annie was so nervous that she missed her first shot. She was embarrassed when she saw that Coach Jackson had seen her.

Annie grabbed her rebound and dribbled to the next basket. She made that one, but she already felt like she had screwed herself up.

For the rest of the tryout that day, things just didn't seem to be working right for Annie. She dropped easy passes and missed shots. And to make matters worse, it seemed like every time she made a mistake, Coach Jackson was watching.

When five o'clock finally rolled around, Annie was tired. She was sweating and exhausted as she headed into the locker room. Emma and Megan jogged over to join her.

As they opened the door to walk in, Annie said, "Emma, you had a really good tryout. I saw you block Dani's shot."

"I was horrible," said Megan. "Did you see me dribble off my foot?"

"I wasn't so great either," said Annie.

"Tomorrow has to be better, right?" asked Megan as the girls changed back into their school clothes. "I mean, I can't get any worse, can I?"

"We were all nervous. I didn't see anyone having a great tryout," said Emma.

"You did. You did everything right. I know you'll make the team," said Annie.

But then she thought, I just don't know if I will.

Chapter 4
JUST OKAY

As Annie walked in the back door of her house that night, she was greeted by one of her favorite smells. Her dad was in the kitchen, stirring a big pot full of bubbling tomato sauce.

"Your homemade spaghetti sauce! Thanks, Dad!" Annie said.

"You're welcome, Annie. I figured you'd be hungry," her dad said. "Are you ready for dinner?"

"Yeah, I guess so," said Annie. She dropped her backpack by the door and sank into a chair.

Her mom walked into the kitchen and put Jack in his high chair. When she saw Annie at the table, Mom asked, "Annie, how did tryouts go?"

"It was okay," Annie said.

"Just okay?" asked her dad. He set a big bowl of salad on the table.

"Yeah," Annie replied. She spread her napkin out on her lap.

"What did you think about the new coach?" her mom asked.

"She's okay," replied Annie.

"Honey, what's wrong?" asked her dad. He looked worried.

"Nothing," said Annie. "I'm just tired, I guess."

Her dad took a tray of garlic bread from the oven and joined the family at the table.

Annie's mom was frowning. Annie pretended she didn't notice. She filled her plate and dug in.

"Well, how did Emma and Megan do?" Mom asked.

"Okay," said Annie between mouthfuls of spaghetti and garlic bread. She was eating really quickly so that she wouldn't be able to talk. She didn't want to tell her parents that after how hard she'd practiced all summer, tryouts had been awful.

After dinner, Annie went upstairs to her room. She had a lot of homework to do before she could go to sleep.

Homework was a struggle that night. She kept going over the tryout in her head.

She couldn't stop thinking about the missed shots and the dropped passes. And she kept seeing the look on Sarah's face when she almost ran into her during laps.

It was hard to concentrate on math and American history. It was hard to think about anything, really, because the tryout had been so disappointing.

Annie didn't finish her homework until after ten o'clock that night. As she pulled on her pajamas, she thought ahead to the next day's tryout.

Tuesday had to go better. If it didn't, she would be cut on Wednesday for sure.

Even though she was really tired, it took Annie a long time to fall asleep.

When her alarm went off the next morning, Annie could barely get out of bed. Her muscles were sore. It hurt to sit up.

She managed to swing her legs over the edge of the bed. Then she slowly walked to the bathroom.

She turned the shower on hot. In the shower, she did her best to stretch out her aching muscles.

When she got out, she felt a little better. Walking wasn't as painful.

After Annie was dressed, she gathered her homework from the night before and stuffed everything into her backpack. Then she headed down to breakfast. Her mom and Jack were already in the kitchen.

"Nee!" cried Jack with a grin.

"Hi, Jack," said Annie.

"So, are you going to tell me how tryouts went yesterday?" asked her mom.

Annie frowned. She knew she should tell her mom. "It was bad," she said.

"Honey, I'm sure the tryout wasn't as bad as you think it was," Mom said.

Annie shook her head. "I missed layups, Mom!" she said. "I'm usually so good at them. And I was so nervous I couldn't hang onto the ball. Emma was good, but Megan was even worse than I was."

Annie stopped and took a deep breath. Then she continued, "I'm afraid I'm going to be cut again. And Sarah was mean, as usual. I almost ran into her during laps. She made me so nervous, and I just kept screwing up."

"Honey, we talked about this," her mom said. "You practiced really hard and made so much progress. Forget about Sarah. Concentrate on your game and you'll do just fine."

Feeling a little better, Annie collected her things and got into the car.

After school, Annie, Emma, and Megan found themselves back in the locker room. It seemed unusually quiet. Then Annie realized that even Sarah and Dani were silent. They weren't making fun of anyone. They weren't laughing. In fact, they weren't even talking to each other.

Megan and Emma noticed too. "They can't be as nervous as I am, can they?" asked Megan.

"Well, they should be!" whispered Emma, afraid of being overheard. "Did you guys see them yesterday? Sarah was awful. It didn't even seem like she cared!"

"It seems like they care today," said Annie, lacing up her shoe.

When they were all ready, Annie and her friends headed out into the gym. Coach Jackson greeted them. "Good afternoon, girls!" she said. "Grab a ball and shoot around for a few minutes." She smiled.

Emma leaned over and took a ball from the blue wire cage by the gym door. She passed it to Megan, who was standing under the basket nearby.

Megan caught the pass, took one dribble to get out from underneath the rim, made a short shot, and missed.

Annie glanced at Coach Jackson, who was watching Megan over her clipboard. Fortunately, Megan didn't notice that the coach was watching.

Over the next fifteen minutes, the rest of the girls trickled in. Soon, the gym was full of yelling girls and bouncing basketballs. Today, Sarah and Dani were actually out of the locker room on time.

After they ran laps, the girls gathered in the middle of the gym. All of them were out of breath. Running laps always made Annie's muscles feel good

Coach Jackson smiled at them. "We're going to do a drill now to test your endurance," she said. "I call it Dig Deep."

She showed the girls how the drill would go. Then it was time to begin.

Soon, it was Annie's turn. She sprinted up the sideline, shuffled across the half-court line, and ran backward down the other sideline. Then she shuffled halfway across the court. She ran as fast as she could up the middle of the court toward the opposite basket. Finally, she caught Coach Jackson's pass and dribbled in for a layup.

Annie was concentrating so hard that she forgot to be nervous for a while. It was the most tiring drill she had ever run. But she made all of her layups, and she didn't trip once.

Megan made two of her three shots, but dropped the coach's pass on the last run. Annie saw Sarah point and laugh with Dani. But Megan didn't seem to care.

The rest of Tuesday's tryout was much better for Annie.

She felt confident. Her passes hit their marks and her shots went in.

The girls smiled and joked together as they changed after the tryout. When they left the locker room that night, they were all in a better mood, even though Megan's tryout hadn't gone well.

The next day was the first round of cuts. Last year, all three girls had made it through the first round — but they'd been cut at the second round.

Annie was terrified that the same thing would happen this year.

Chapter 6
FIRST CUT

On Wednesday afternoon, Annie and her friends walked toward the locker room. Annie was starting to feel like things were going a lot better this year.

She felt a lot more confident. It helped that Sarah and her friends didn't scare her like they used to.

Annie was worried about Megan, though. So far, neither of her tryouts had been very good.

"Are you guys nervous today?" Annie asked.

"I feel pretty good," replied Emma. "All that practice this summer is really paying off. I'm sure it helps that I'm like the Jolly Green Giant, though." She laughed.

Megan took a deep breath and said, "I think I'm getting cut."

"No you aren't!" exclaimed Annie.

Emma said, "Megan, you're a great basketball player. Don't talk like that."

The three friends dressed quickly. Then they headed into the gym.

Coach Jackson told them that they'd be running a timed shooting drill. The girls had one minute to score as many points as possible from five different spots on the floor.

Annie got second place, right behind Sarah. Emma was third. Megan finished somewhere in the middle.

At the end of the tryout, Coach Miller blew her whistle. All of the girls quieted down. "As you know, some of you will be cut today," Coach Miller said. "We'll have the list posted on the wall by the drinking fountain when you're done showering and changing. Thank you for all of your hard work this week."

Back in the locker room, the three friends showered quickly. They changed back into their school clothes.

Finally, they headed back into the gym. Annie, Megan, and Emma slowly walked over to the list on the wall. They stepped up to the list and looked for their names.

Emma
Lisa
Caitlyn
Annie
Sarah
Dani
Jenna
Elizabeth
Siena

Emma let out a sigh of relief. Her name was first on the list. Annie saw her own name just a few lines down. Sarah and Dani had made it through the cut, too.

When Annie looked again, though, Megan's name wasn't there. Annie's stomach dropped. Emma gasped.

They both turned to look at Megan, who shrugged and said, "It's okay, guys. Really. I'll talk to you later. My mom's waiting."

Chapter 7
NO MORE MEGAN

At home that night, Annie was
exhausted. She had almost forgotten how
much work basketball could be. She was
glad she didn't have any homework to do
that night. She was just too tired.

After dinner, she took Jack from his high
chair and into the living room. They played
an exciting game of peek-a-boo for a while.
Then Jack started to get sleepy and Annie's
mom came to take him to bed.

"Mom, did Megan's mom tell you that she got cut today?" Annie asked.

"Yes, she did," Annie's mom replied. "She also said that Megan was okay with it. Honey, I don't think Megan wanted to make the team."

"What do you mean? Why not?" Annie asked. She felt shocked.

"Megan's mom told me that Megan doesn't want to play basketball anymore. She's just been afraid to tell you. She thought you'd be mad," Mom said.

"Oh," said Annie. "I'm not mad. Why would I be mad?"

"I don't know, honey," Mom said. "I guess you'll have to talk to Megan about that tomorrow."

Annie yawned. Her mom smiled.

"Go to bed, Annie," Mom said. "Tomorrow's another big day for you. Sweet dreams."

Annie slowly walked upstairs to her room, thinking about what her mom had said. She had to talk to Megan. But first, she had to talk to Emma.

* * *

Emma was waiting outside the school when Annie arrived the next morning.

"Emma!" shouted Annie. "Megan's mom told my mom that Megan didn't want to play! She didn't want us to be mad, so she tried out anyway."

"What? Why would we be mad?" asked Emma, looking a little hurt.

"I don't know. But when we see her, we need to tell her we're not," Annie said.

They found Megan in the hall by her locker. "Hey, Megan," said Annie. "Didn't you want to try out this year?"

Megan took a deep breath and replied, "No. But you guys were so excited. I thought you'd be mad."

"We're not mad," said Emma. "But why didn't you want to try out?"

"I don't really like playing basketball that much anymore," Megan said. "I still like watching it. I just don't love playing it like I used to."

"That's okay, Megan," said Annie. "We're not mad. But you have to promise to come to all of the games and cheer really loudly. Deal?"

"Deal," said Megan, looking relieved.

* * *

At tryouts that afternoon, the first thing they did was a layup drill. It was the same drill they'd done the first day of tryouts, but this time, they had to shoot with their left hands.

Annie took a deep breath before dribbling in. She shot the ball up, but it hit the underside of the rim with a loud thunk. She felt her face turn red, but she quickly grabbed her ball and continued on.

She concentrated hard and made the rest of her layups, but she was afraid the damage had already been done. Annie was frustrated and exhausted at the end of the day.

Finally, it was over. Coach Jackson told them that by the time they were dressed, the list would be posted in the gym.

Nervously, Annie showered and changed. She and Emma again walked out of the locker room and into the gym.

Once again, the list was posted on the wall by the drinking fountain. And just like the day before, both of their names were near the top of the list.

But Annie couldn't shake the feeling that just like last year, she'd be cut from the team. Dani and Sarah would make it and she wouldn't. It would be last year all over again.

Chapter 8
GOOD SIGNS

When Annie looked out her bedroom window on Friday morning, it was bright and sunny outside. She decided to take it as a good sign.

After she got ready for school, she headed downstairs. In the kitchen, Annie poured herself a bowl of cereal and a glass of orange juice. Jack was in his high chair, and their mom was reading the paper.

"Feeling okay, honey?" her mom asked.

"Yeah, actually," Annie replied. "I have a good feeling about today."

She took a drink of juice before continuing. "I'm sure Emma will make the team," Annie went on. "And I really want to make the team too. But I guess it would be okay if I didn't."

Her mom smiled. "Well, just do your best today," she told Annie. "And don't count yourself out yet."

"I'm not. Can we go soon? I want to talk to Emma and Megan before class," Annie explained.

"Go!" cried Jack. Annie smiled at him.

At school, Emma and Megan were waiting for her just inside the front doors. They looked like they knew something she didn't.

"Annie, guess what!" squealed Megan as soon as she saw Annie. She had a huge smile on her face.

Annie walked over. "What's up, Megan?" she asked.

Megan said, "Coach Jackson asked me if I would be the team manager! I'll get to keep score and go to all the practices and games. Isn't that fantastic? I mean, I still love basketball, even if I don't like playing it very much anymore."

"That's awesome! Now I just have to make the team," said Annie. She felt the nervous feeling in her stomach again.

"Don't worry, Annie. You've worked really hard. You're on the team for sure," said Emma confidently.

* * *

When the bell sounded at the end of the day, Annie wasn't worried or scared anymore.

Her fear was gone. Now she just wanted to prove to herself that she was good enough to make the team.

She wanted to prove that she had tried hard enough. She had put in the effort all summer and had given everything she had at every tryout.

When Annie and Emma stepped onto the court, Annie knew what she would do. She would try her best, and she would make the team.

Chapter 9
HEART AND SOUL

When the tryout began, Coach Jackson showed them a passing drill.

The girls lined up in three lines. Annie and Emma were first in two of the three lines. Sarah was first in the other line. She glared at Annie. But Annie ignored her.

Annie had the ball. She took a deep breath and passed it to Emma. Then she ran around behind Emma as Emma passed the ball to Sarah.

All three girls ran down the court toward the other basket. Sarah passed the ball back to Annie, and Annie made the layup.

"Great!" yelled Coach Jackson. "Great teamwork, girls!"

The team ran the passing drill for the next half hour. Annie started to feel great. Her heart was pounding from working so hard, but most importantly, she was having a great time. She almost forgot that it could be her last time on the court that year.

Coach Jackson blew her whistle. "Okay, girls," she said. "Now we're going to play a game called Heart and Soul. It will help Coach Miller and me make our decisions."

Annie already knew the game. She had learned it at camp one year. It was a kind of three-on-two.

The girls were split into two teams. One had two players, and one had three. The object of the game was for the team of two to steal the ball or get the rebound from the team of three.

The team of two would take the ball the other way. A girl from the other team would join them. Then the other team, which now had two players, would play defense.

Annie and Emma took defensive positions on the court while three girls in jerseys dribbled up the floor. Coach Jackson blew her whistle and the game began.

Annie loved the game. It was fun. That meant she could relax and play her favorite sport. She didn't feel nervous anymore. She was just happy to be playing basketball.

She was surprised when Coach Jackson blew her whistle to stop the game.

"Okay, girls, that's it," the coach said. "You all did a great job. Please go into the locker room, shower, and change. Then come back out here and have a seat against the bleachers."

With a small smile to herself, Annie walked into the locker room. She felt good about her tryout. When she glanced at Emma, she was also smiling.

Back in the gym, Coach Jackson waited until all of the girls had returned. Then she said, "Thank you again for all of your hard work. The following girls will be on this year's seventh-grade basketball team. Annie, Mariah, Emma, Melanie, Sarah, Leslie, Jenna . . ."

She did it! She made the team! Annie and Emma squealed and hugged.

As Annie left that night, Coach Jackson walked up to her. "Annie, can I talk to you for a second?" she asked.

"Sure, Coach," Annie said, feeling confused. "What's up?"

"I just wanted to tell you that I'm really proud of you," Coach Jackson said. "You're exactly what I look for in a basketball player. No matter what happened, you kept playing. You gave everything, all the time."

"Thanks," Annie said shyly. She smiled.

Coach Jackson went on, "Making the team is just the beginning. I think you have a lot of potential, and it was really obvious today. Annie, you played with your heart and soul."

ABOUT THE AUTHOR

Val Priebe lives in Minneapolis, Minnesota with her two crazy wiener dogs, Bruce and Lily. Besides writing books, she loves to spend her time reading, knitting, cooking, and coaching basketball. Her favorite drill to coach is Heart and Soul, because even though she's short, she can play too!

ABOUT THE ILLUSTRATOR

When Tuesday Mourning was a little girl, she knew she wanted to be an artist when she grew up. Now, she is an illustrator who lives in Knoxville, Tennessee. She especially loves illustrating books for kids and teenagers. When she isn't illustrating, Tuesday loves spending time with her husband, who is an actor, and their son, Atticus.

GLOSSARY

aching (AY-king)—hurting

concentrate (KON-suhn-trate)—to focus your thoughts and attention on something

confident (KON-fuh-fuhnt)—having a strong belief in your own abilities

drill (DRIL)—a method of learning by repeating something

endurance (en-DUR-uhnss)—an endurance drill tests someone's patience and strength

lap (LAP)—one time around something

layup (LAY-uhp)—a shot made with one hand, from near the basket

potential (puh-TEN-shuhl)—what one is capable of achieving in the future

rebound (REE-bownd)—if you catch a basketball after it has bounced off the basket, you have caught a rebound

roster (ROSS-tur)—a list of team members

stressful (STRESS)—something that causes worry or pressure

tryout (TRYE-out)—a test to make a team

MORE ABOUT:

The first season of the Women's National Basketball Association (the WNBA) began in June 1997.

Since the beginning of the WNBA, there have been a lot of firsts for women's basketball.

* First player signed: Sheryl Swoopes on October 23, 1996. Sheryl also had her own Nike basketball shoes, just like Michael Jordan!

* First WNBA president: Val Ackerman

* First WNBA MVP (Most Valuable Player): Cynthia Cooper

The WNBA uses a special basketball designed by Spalding. It is orange and oatmeal in color, and is 28.5 inches in circumference. That's just one inch smaller than the ball used by NBA teams!

THE WOMEN'S NATIONAL BASKETBALL ASSOCIATION

The WNBA's first championship team was the Houston Comets. The Comets beat the New York Liberty 65–51 in the championship game. In fact, the Comets went on to win the championship each year for the next three years, making them four-time champions!

When the WNBA got its start, there were eight teams. There are now 16 teams in the WNBA, and games are shown on ESPN, ESPN2, and NBC during the summer months.

The WNBA has been around for over 10 years and has given many women the chance to achieve their dreams of playing professional basketball.

DISCUSSION QUESTIONS

1. Have you ever tried out for something? What did you try out for? What was the experience like? Talk about it.

2. Sarah and Dani are mean to everyone! Without naming names, do you know anyone who acts like they do? What are some good ways to handle bullies?

3. In this book, Megan decides she doesn't want to play basketball anymore, but she doesn't tell Emma and Annie about her decision. What would you do if you felt like Megan? How would you handle it? Talk about different ways to tell your friends.

WRITING PROMPTS

1. In this book, Annie, Megan, and Emma are best friends who also play basketball together. What do you and your best friends do together? Write about your favorite thing to do with your friends.

2. When Annie is upset about how tryouts went, her mom tries to make her feel better. Is there an adult in your life who makes you feel better when you're feeling bad? Write about that person.

3. Have you ever tried out for something but not gotten the result you wanted? What happened? How did you handle it?

Ella and Laura can't believe it when two of the meanest girls from a rival volleyball team switch to their team. They decide to give the new girls a chance, but before long it's clear that Beth and Gretchen don't plan to be good teammates.